Rosie the Runaway Pony

Rosie didn't feel like staying in the field with stroppy old Nellie all morning.

She gave the gate a nudge with her nose. Ever since the old gate had been replaced, the catch didn't always click shut properly. Sometimes if you gave it a really firm push . . .

Rosie tried again, and this time, the gate clicked open. "Yes!" Rosie whinnied.

Titles in Jenny Dale's PONY TALES™ series

Sam the School Pony
Charlie the Champion Pony
Lottie the Little Pony
Shadow the Secret Pony
Rosie the Runaway Pony
Willow the Wild Pony

MACMILLAN CHILDREN'S BOOKS

Special thanks to Gwyneth Rees
For Eve, Cameron and Anna

First published 2000 by Macmillan Children's Books
a division of Macmillan Publishers Limited
20 New Wharf Road, London N1 9RR
Basingstoke and Oxford
www.panmacmillan.com

Associated companies throughout the world

Created by Working Partners Limited
London W6 0QT

ISBN 0 330 37473 7

5 7 9 8 6

A CIP catalogue record for this book is available from
the British Library.

Typeset by SX Composing DTP, Rayleigh, Essex
Printed and bound in Great Britain by Mackays of Chatham plc, Kent

C'est déjà un bon départ, mais à l'intérieur de vous, dans votre façon de voir, de vous voir. Nous avons répété des centaines de fois : l'unicité dans la dualité que vous êtes. Qu'est-ce que cela voulait dire ? Vivez seul et vous serez seul, mais vous ne serez jamais seul si vous comprenez que vous êtes déjà deux ; et nous pourrions dire : vous êtes déjà trois. C'est cela qu'il faut vivre. Brisez le cycle actuel, faites-vous un peu plus plaisir, cessez de regarder les ravages et vous vous verrez. Des changements ? Il y en aura certainement, mais peut-être pas dans le sens que vous les avez imaginés cependant. Le chaos dans votre monde humain actuel, c'est beaucoup plus dans la parole ; et l'harmonie est beaucoup plus dans le silence. Prenez le temps d'entendre en vous. Elle est déçue ? Réconfortez-la, faites-lui voir une chance qu'elle aurait d'être avec vous. En d'autres termes, il est grand temps que vous appreniez à vous convaincre que vous vivez et que vous avez un but à atteindre. Si vous ne le faites pas, vous ne l'aurez pas. Cependant, vous avez de bonnes chances de réussir. *(Les chercheurs d'étoiles, III, 17-11-1996)*

Si l'Âme aide la forme, commen fait-il qu'on voit certaines fami où se sont groupées ensemble des formes sont toutes dures, c'est-à-dire que ça mal, que les enfants sont gâtés, etc. Est- que les Âmes ont choisi de mauvaise formes ?

Nous avons répondu à cette question à plusieurs reprises. Nous avons dit que les Âmes ont perdu le contrôle des formes et nous avons souvent répété : qui se ressemble s'assemble. Si ces gens apprennent à vivre dans le malheur et y trouvent du bonheur, c'est ce qu'ils sont à apprendre. Rappelez-vous toujours que la dimension des uns n'est pas nécessairement celle des autres. Soyez seulement heureux de ne pas être avec eux ; c'est leur réalité, pas la vôtre. Ce qu'ils auront à apprendre dans cela sera leur leçon de vie et si cela peut vous aider à ne pas faire d'erreur, tant mieux. *(Harmonie, IV, 16-02-1991)*

Est-il possible qu'un enfant aille jusqu'à être malade pour permettre

années parce que vous aurez toujours peur, vous aurez toujours des craintes, et ce ne sera plus facile de vivre votre vie à vous ; c'est la même chose pour le conjoint. Il y a des choses qui ne sont pas toujours agréables mais qui doivent être faites dans le but d'aider vraiment, de force s'il le faut. *(Les chercheurs d'étoiles, II, 20-10-1996)*

Est-ce qu'il y a une dette à payer dans un suicide ?

Pour cela, il faut connaître le pourquoi du suicide, l'Âme, la forme qu'elle avait, ainsi que les influences vécues. En règle générale, ce choix que font les formes pour en finir avec la vie est directement relié à un manque d'amour, de partage et de compréhension, ainsi qu'à l'oubli de la part de ceux qui vivent autour d'elles. Sachant cela, comment voulez-vous punir une Âme qui ne peut maîtriser une forme incapable de maîtriser sa sensibilité, pour trop d'amour qu'elle n'a pu communiquer ? Les Âmes quittent généralement les formes au moment exact où le conscient perd la réalité consciente de sa forme. L'imagination poussée peut devenir une fausse réalité. *(Les pèlerins, I, 27-01-1990)*

Pourquoi des gens qu'on aime beaucoup veulent-ils se détruire et culpabiliser leur entourage ?

Parce qu'ils ne s'aiment pas eux-mêmes. Et comme il leur faut justifier leurs agissements pour arriver à commettre un suicide, ils doivent associer des gens à leur malheur. Donc, ils adoptent des comportements en conséquence. Vous allez vous rendre compte que ces gens ne se sont jamais exprimés et, lorsqu'ils l'ont fait, c'était dans la colère. *(Renaissance, III, 09-11-1991)*

Quelles sont les conséquences du suicide pour l'Âme ? Pourquoi les gens décident-ils de se suicider ?

La croyance généralisée est que ces personnes ne s'aiment pas, mais c'est tout le contraire. Ce sont des personnes tellement conscientes de ne pas aimer ce qu'elles vivent actuellement que leur seule façon de s'aimer est de quitter ce monde. Donc, ce sont des gens qui prennent conscience qu'ils ne s'aiment pas, mais qui savent faire la différence entre cet état et un autre où ils pourraient s'aimer. Comme ils ne voient pas de moyens de changer ces états, ils deviennent tellement convaincus que rien ne les arrête. Ce qui fera la différence, c'est le temps que vous prendrez, ou l'instant où cela se passera pour les convaincre du contraire. Cela fera une différence. Bien souvent, il est trop tard ; leur idée est déjà faite. Cela, c'est au niveau des formes. La prochaine fois que vous entendrez parler d'une personne qui s'est suicidée, dites-vous une seule chose : elle s'aimait probablement un peu trop pour vivre ce qu'elle vivait. Ce n'est pas toujours compréhensible de la part des autres. Donc, regardez le milieu, les gens qui l'entouraient. Y avait-il suffisamment d'ouverture ? Était-ce perceptible ? Pour certains, Noël se fête une fois par année ; pour d'autres, c'est tous les jours. Pour certains, des cadeaux sont des objets ; pour d'autres, c'est dire « je t'aime ». Cela aussi a des conséquences au niveau de l'Âme. Très souvent, cette Âme est mise de côté par ses pairs, comme si elle n'avait pas fait tout ce qu'il fallait, comme si elle n'avait pas laissé percevoir ce qu'elle était. Habituellement, à moins que ces Âmes ne puissent démontrer qu'elles ont tout fait, elles sont mises de côté, le temps d'observer encore. Elles sont mises de côté avec d'autres qui ont vécu la même chose, pour que cela ne se refasse pas, pour apprendre à mieux reprogrammer les formes. Bien souvent, plus de 90 % des fois, elles se blâment elles-mêmes. Effectivement, il y a des conséquences. Cependant, il faut aussi regarder autre chose, ce que cela laisse derrière. Dans certains cas, ce sont des familles qui se réunissent. Vous savez pour quelle raison ? Parce que, comme dans des guerres, là où vous avez appris le plus, c'est quand il y a eu douleur, quand il y a eu souffrance. En

Jenny Dale's PONY TALES™

Rosie the Runaway Pony

by Jenny Dale

Illustrated by Frank Rodgers

A Working Partners Book

MACMILLAN CHILDREN'S BOOKS

Special thanks to Gwyneth Rees
For Eve, Cameron and Anna

First published 2000 by Macmillan Children's Books
a division of Macmillan Publishers Limited
20 New Wharf Road, London N1 9RR
Basingstoke and Oxford
www.panmacmillan.com

Associated companies throughout the world

Created by Working Partners Limited
London W6 0QT

ISBN 0 330 37473 7

5 7 9 8 6

A CIP catalogue record for this book is available from
the British Library.

Typeset by SX Composing DTP, Rayleigh, Essex
Printed and bound in Great Britain by Mackays of Chatham plc, Kent

Chapter One

"See you later, Rosie," Kay White said, excitedly. It was the first day of term and she had stopped on her way to school to give her pony an apple. Rosie loved apples and she could eat her way through lots and lots of them if she was given the chance.

Kay patted her one last time and shouted goodbye to Nellie, the family's other pony.

Nellie was standing further away in the field, with her back turned towards the gate. She was getting old. She always tried to stay as far away as possible from the road when school was about to start. She didn't like the noise the children made as they passed by.

Rosie couldn't understand Nellie not liking noise. *She* liked things to be as noisy and exciting as possible. She loved to watch the children pass by under her nose. In fact, she always thrust out her nose as far she could over the top of the hedge, in order to see everything that was happening.

All the children in the village knew Rosie, and Rosie would have happily gone to school with them, if she could.

Kay banged the gate shut in a hurry as she spotted her friend, Jessica, walking down the road.

"Hi, Kay! Hi, Rosie!" Jessica called out, swinging her school bag up on to her shoulder. "Hey, what do you think our new teacher will be like?"

Rosie watched the two girls disappear up the road towards the school.

After several other children had passed by and given her nose a pat, Rosie heard the sound of a bell ringing. She knew what that meant. It meant there would be no more children, and that Kay wouldn't be back for ages.

Rosie didn't feel like staying in the field with stroppy old Nellie all morning.

She gave the gate a nudge with her nose. Ever since the old gate had been replaced, the catch didn't always click shut properly. Sometimes if you gave it a really firm push . . .

Rosie tried again, and this time, the gate clicked open. "Yes!" Rosie whinnied.

Nellie turned her head at the noise and neighed crossly at Rosie, "Where are you going *this* time?"

"Just exploring again!" Rosie neighed back. "Why don't you

come with me? There's a pond behind the post office, full of nice weedy things!"

But Rosie knew that Nellie wouldn't. Even when the gate was wide open, Nellie never left the field.

"If you leave hoof marks in that garden everyone will know it's you, and you'll get into trouble,"

Nellie snorted. "Anyway, you shouldn't eat strange weeds. They could be poisonous!"

"Don't worry. I won't eat anything poisonous!" Rosie neighed back, as she headed out onto the lane. Rosie liked the sound her hooves made on the tarmac.

"Some poisonous plants don't *look* poisonous," Nellie whinnied after her, "but they are!"

Rosie pretended she hadn't heard, and trotted off towards the village.

In class, Kay thought her new teacher, Miss Hunter, seemed quite nice.

Miss Hunter had just finished

telling them about the big school in London where she used to teach. Kay was glad that she didn't live in London. It sounded too busy and noisy, and it would be very hard to find a field for Rosie and Nellie. Not that Rosie would mind moving somewhere busy and noisy, Kay thought with a smile. Rosie always wanted to be in the middle of things.

It was warm in the classroom, even though all the windows were open.

Kay heard the sound of hooves on the lane and looked to see who was out riding. "Oh no!" she cried, standing up.

"What's wrong?" Miss Hunter asked her.

"It's Rosie," Kay gasped, pointing out of the window.

Kay's classmates started to laugh.

"Rosie?" Miss Hunter asked, looking confused.

Everybody in the class started talking at once.

"It's her pony, Miss!" one of

them shouted. "She's always escaping and going into the village!"

"She ended up in my gran's garden last month, Miss!" said another.

"My mum caught her drinking out of our fish pond last week, Miss!" said Jessica, giggling.

"My dad's always getting phoned up by people complaining that she's in their gardens!" Sam Hughes added, from his seat behind Kay. "My dad's the village police sergeant, Miss. He says that most of the unlawful entry in this village isn't done by burglars – it's done by Rosie!"

Miss Hunter looked like she was about to say something when

there was a knock on the door.

Mr Gibb, the school caretaker, put his head into the classroom. "Rosie's heading for the village again," he said, shaking his head and trying not to smile. "I called out to her but the little madam flicked her tail at me and speeded up. You'd better come with me, Kay. If that's OK with you, Miss Hunter?"

"Well . . ." Miss Hunter looked like she didn't know *what* was OK in this situation.

"It's what we usually do," Mr Gibb added.

"Well in that case . . ." Miss Hunter waved them out of the room and sat down with a thud in her seat.

"Goodness me!" she said as Kay was leaving. "I had no idea that living in the country could be so hectic!"

"Would you look at that!" Mr Gibb gasped as he and Kay reached the school gate.

Rosie had stopped at the end of a driveway further up the road. Her head was inside a large box that had been left just outside the gate. Beside the box was a big sign that read:

APPLES FOR SALE
10P EACH
PLEASE LEAVE MONEY IN BOX

"Oh no!" Kay exclaimed.

"I hope you've got plenty of money in your pocket!" Mr Gibb said, laughing.

Chapter Two

"Now you stay in your field today like a good pony," Kay told Rosie sternly, as she left her the next morning. She had ridden Rosie before school, given her a good rub-down and fed her. Hopefully, after yesterday's adventure, Rosie would be too tired to try and escape again! Anyway, Kay made sure she shut the gate really carefully this time.

After Kay had gone, Rosie stood at the hedge to wait for the other children to pass by. Nellie was up in the far corner of the field as usual.

"Look, it's Rosie!" an excited voice shouted.

Rosie craned her neck over the hedge to be patted on the nose by two boys. They were in Kay's class at school.

"Wasn't it funny yesterday when Rosie escaped?" one of them said. "I wish Rosie would escape again this morning. We're doing maths first thing and it's going to be so boring!"

"Couldn't we sort of *help* her to escape?" his friend suggested.

"We'd better not . . ." said the other boy.

"Come on! It'll be a laugh!" said his friend. "No one will know it was us. Rosie's always escaping!"

As Rosie watched, she couldn't believe her luck! The two boys

were opening the gate for her!

"Come on, Rosie! Follow us!" they called out, as they ran off up the road.

Rosie trotted out through the gate, but she didn't follow the boys. She had gone that way yesterday. Today, she felt like exploring in the other direction. She would take the road that led out of the village.

"Kay's going to be really cross with you!" Nellie neighed.

Rosie snorted. "No, she won't!" Kay never got *really* cross with her. Nellie was the one who got most annoyed whenever Rosie escaped from their field. Honestly, you'd think *Nellie* was Rosie's owner, the way she carried on!

Rosie headed for the row of houses ahead of her. She saw a large van parked outside one of them.

"Ooh, a horsebox," Rosie neighed. She liked horseboxes because they usually meant she was being taken somewhere interesting. Rosie loved exploring new places.

There didn't seem to be any people in charge of this horsebox, though. Rosie trotted up the ramp and stopped just inside the door. She was surprised to find all sorts of clutter in there. But there would just about be room for her to make herself comfortable – if she got past this thing that looked like a small tree.

There was a loud clatter as the tree thing fell over and hung half out of the horsebox.

"Hey! Watch that coat stand! Who's in there?" called a gruff voice.

Rosie turned round, knocking over something else in the process. She stuck her head out of the back of the horsebox to see who had shouted. Two men were coming towards her.

"Hello!" she neighed. "If you're going somewhere interesting, can I come too? I'm sure Kay won't really mind!"

"But I *know* I shut it properly today!" Kay wailed, as she stood by the open gate to Rosie's field.

Jessica had been late on her way to school that morning. She had seen that the gate to the field was open and raised the alarm.

Mr Gibb had stopped mending things in the school basement, and come with Kay to investigate. "We'd better go and see if she went into the village," he said.

But as they set off in the direction of the village, Nellie began to neigh and snort and gallop along the inside of the hedge.

"What's the matter, Nellie?" Kay asked. It was most unlike her mother's old horse to get so worked up.

Now that she had Kay's attention, Nellie turned and trotted in the opposite direction.

"Nellie, what are you trying to tell us? Are you saying that Rosie went in *that* direction?" Kay looked at the row of houses that stood on the main road leading out of the village. She could just make out a large removal van parked outside the end house. She decided to go and ask if the removal men had seen Rosie.

As she and Mr Gibb got closer, Kay heard the removal men grunting crossly at another man who had a map in his hand.

"Don't bother us asking for directions now," one of the removal men growled. "Can't you see we're up to our eyes in it? There's a bloomin' pony in our van!"

He pointed inside the removal van, just as Rosie turned round to make herself more comfortable and sent a box clattering to the ground.

"Rosie!" Kay gasped.

Rosie was so excited to hear Kay's voice that she turned again, and both removal men yelled out in alarm.

"If that's your pony, then you get her out of there – and hurry up about it!" the gruffest removal man snapped at Kay.

Luckily, Rosie didn't need much persuasion to leave the van now that Kay was here.

"I'm really sorry," Kay said to the men. "Rosie loves going into horseboxes and I suppose this looked like a horsebox to her."

The removal men looked very cross.

"Yeah, well, it's not, and we've got a job to get on with!" one of them grunted.

The man with the map seemed to have forgotten about wanting directions. He seemed more interested in Rosie now. "Do you have to take your pony far?" he asked.

"Oh no," Kay replied. "Just to that field along the lane – the one with our other pony." She pointed out Nellie in the distance.

"What a nice field!" the man exclaimed.

"How odd!" said Kay to Mr Gibb, as they walked with Rosie back to her field. "Why was that man so interested in where Rosie was kept?"

Mr Gibb chuckled. "I don't know," he said. "Perhaps he lives in the city. People who live in the city seem to find all sorts of everyday country things curious!"

Kay laughed, thinking of Miss Hunter.

Chapter Three

That afternoon, Rosie watched as Nellie slowly nibbled at some grass. Rosie sniffed the air and flicked her tail at a buzzy insect. Buzzy insects were tickly if they landed on your back.

In the lane, a large van pulled up outside their gate.

"Ooh, another horsebox!" Rosie whickered. She stamped her front hooves in excitement. Maybe Kay's mum was going to take them somewhere exciting.

"Not every big van is a horsebox, Rosie," Kay had told her sternly that morning. But Rosie was sure that this time she was right. This *was* a horsebox.

It wasn't Mrs White who was driving it, though. Rosie could see a man getting out. She had seen him before. It was the friendly man who had been talking to Kay that morning.

The man walked over to the gate, holding out something that looked like a . . .

Rosie trotted closer. Yes! It *was* a

carrot! Yum!

She cantered over to him. "Thank you very much," she whinnied. "I don't mind if I do!"

As Rosie crunched on the carrot, she saw Nellie watching to see what all the fuss was about. Just then, the man flicked the catch on the gate and pushed it open.

Rosie snorted in delight. "Oh,

what a helpful man you are!"

Nellie trotted closer. "Rosie!" she neighed. "You shouldn't talk to strangers!"

Rosie pretended not to hear her again.

"Look what I've got!" said the man. "A horsebox! Just like that nice horsebox you went inside this morning. Except this time it's all empty – just for you!"

"Stop mucking around, will you?" came a cross voice from the driver's seat at the front of the van. "I don't know why you don't just tie her up and shove her inside!"

"Because she doesn't need to be tied up, do you, my beauty?" the other man answered, stroking

Rosie's back. "This pony will trot into that box without you even asking her to. Watch!" He threw a handful of carrots into the back of the horsebox for Rosie.

Hardly able to believe her luck, Rosie hurried up the ramp, into the horsebox. The inside smelled of hay. It reminded Rosie of when she'd gone with Kay to the next village. There had been lots of jumps set up for her to try, and lots of other ponies to snort at. How exciting!

At that moment, Nellie came galloping down the field towards the gate.

"We don't need an old nag like you, I'm afraid," the man told Nellie. Then he crashed the door

of the horsebox shut. "OK, let's go!" he called.

Rosie heard the passenger door at the front slam shut and the engine start up.

Nellie was making a lot of noise outside. Rosie couldn't make out what she was whinnying about. But she soon stopped thinking about Nellie as the horsebox took off along the road at a furious speed.

This wasn't what Rosie was used to at all. When Kay's mum or dad was driving they went at a very careful pace along the country lanes. What was going on?

Kay noticed Nellie standing by the gate as she turned the corner on her way home from school. That was odd. Normally Nellie stood as far back in her field as possible when the schoolchildren were passing. It was Rosie who usually stood waiting at the gate.

Kay looked around the rest of the field to see where Rosie was. But apart from Nellie, the field was empty. And as she got closer,

Kay could see that the catch on the gate was open again!

Kay felt the sick feeling in her stomach that she always got whenever Rosie went missing. She hurried home, hoping that her mum or dad would be able to come and help her look for Rosie.

As she turned into the driveway, her dad's Land Rover pulled up.

But before Kay could tell him that Rosie had run away again, he said, "I've just seen Rosie in that field with the apple tree she likes."

Kay sighed with relief. At least Rosie was safe. "Can we go and fetch her?" she asked.

Her dad nodded. "Let's just go and tell your mum what we're up to."

Kay wasn't too worried now. Rosie would be sitting down under her favourite apple tree having a nice rest, just like she always did after she'd pigged out on apples.

"Why on earth does that pony keep running off?" Mrs White said, frowning, when she heard. "She has a perfectly nice field of her own."

"Rosie has a *mind* of her own, too, I'm afraid," Mr White replied, smiling.

Kay and her dad walked to the field with the apple tree. It had become one of Rosie's favourite places to visit since she discovered apples were beginning to fall from the tree.

"There she is!" Mr White pointed.

Kay stared hard at the pony in the field. "That's not Rosie," she said.

Her dad looked again. "You're right!" he said, in surprise. "It isn't! That pony does look a lot like her, though."

"Yes, but it *isn't* her, Dad!" Kay protested in alarm. "So Rosie is still missing. Where is she?"

Just then a girl came along and stopped at the gate. "Is something wrong?" she asked. She was a year or two older than Kay and she was dressed as if she was about to go riding.

"We thought that was Rosie, my daughter's pony," Mr White answered. "She keeps escaping from her field and sometimes she comes here."

"That's my pony – Rosamund," the girl said. "We've just moved here. I'm Amy, by the way."

Kay smiled at Amy. "And I'm Kay," she said. "My pony got into a removal van this morning. Was it yours?"

Amy laughed. "Yes," she replied. "I heard the removal men grumbling about it when I got home from school!"

"I hope she didn't break anything," Kay said. "She thought it was a horsebox."

"No. She just gave the removal men a fright!" Amy replied, grinning.

"You haven't seen a pony that looks like your Rosamund around here, have you?" Mr White asked, looking up and down the road.

Amy shook her head. "No, but my mum saw a horsebox zoom past our house a little while ago. She came out to check on Rosamund, because someone tried to steal her last month.

Rosamund has won loads of prizes, and now she's very valuable," Amy explained.

When she heard this, Kay remembered something. "Oh no!" she gasped.

"What is it?" her dad asked.

"There was a man asking about Rosie this morning," Kay replied. She looked at Amy. "He was standing outside your house. He seemed really interested in Rosie and I told him where Rosie's field was. What if . . . What if he thought Rosie was Rosamund? What if he meant to steal Rosamund but he took Rosie by mistake?"

Chapter Four

Rosie usually loved riding in horseboxes, but this horsebox was travelling far too fast.

There was a gap in the wood where some other pony had kicked the side, and Rosie could see that they were passing the same houses that they'd passed earlier. They seemed to be going round in circles.

From the front of the van, Rosie could hear raised voices.

"I told you we should have got a better map!"

"If you slowed down a bit I might have time to *read* the map properly!"

The louder the men argued, the more worried Rosie became. She neighed loudly and reared up in her box. This seemed to make the two men shout at each other even more.

"I told you we should have tied her up!"

"She'll be fine! Just concentrate on the road, will you?"

Rosie started to stamp her feet

and whinny as loud as she could. She kicked her back hooves against the side of the van. She wanted to be let out!

Suddenly, the vehicle screeched to a halt. Rosie was thrown against the back wall – it hurt and made her angry.

"It's all your fault!" one of the men was shouting at the other.

The men were climbing out of the van. Rosie watched as the door at the back opened. The man she knew from before was standing there with a length of rope.

Rosie lurched forward and reared up as he tried to throw the rope around her. "Oh no you don't!" she whinnied. She kicked

out at him and he yelled in fright, then dodged out of the way.

Rosie pushed past him, leaped out on to the road, and galloped away as fast as she could, snorting with relief. She was free again!

She knew this road! It led to another road that led back to her field. Soon she would be home again!

Kay and her dad had hurried back to the house to fetch the Land Rover. Kay had to bite her lip to stop herself from crying. What if Rosie really had been stolen? What if the people who had stolen her were being cruel to her?

"We'll drive over to the police station," her dad said, gently.

"Maybe someone has reported seeing her."

As they drove past Rosie's field, Kay couldn't bear to look.

Then Mr White laughed. "Look, Kay!" he said.

Kay looked. Rosie was standing on the outside of the gate, waiting to be let in. Nellie was standing on the other side, gently butting Rosie, as if she was telling her off.

"Dad! Rosie's back!" Kay yelled out.

Her dad stopped the Land Rover and Kay jumped out and ran over to Rosie as fast as she could. "Oh, Rosie! I'm so happy to see you!" Kay cried out, hugging her pony hard.

"And I'm certainly glad to be

back!" Rosie snorted.

"Well, it looks like Rosie just ran away again," Mr White said, opening the gate for her.

"Yes!" Rosie neighed in agreement. She *had* run away again. Only this time, she had run away *back home*!

Chapter Five

"Well, I just hope you've learned your lesson," Nellie snorted, after Rosie had told her about her horrible adventure.

Rosie promised that she had.

But every day Rosie couldn't resist nudging the gate to see if it would open. And finally, a week later, she found she was in luck!

Nellie looked up from munching grass. "Where are you going?" she neighed, sharply.

"Don't worry. I won't be going into any more horseboxes. I'm just going to say hello to Rosamund!" Rosie neighed back.

Kay and Amy had been out riding together three times in the past week, so Rosie and Rosamund had become friends.

"You're going to say hello to that apple tree, you mean!" Nellie snorted. "Greedy guts!"

Rosie just swished her tail and kept trotting.

She arrived at Rosamund's field and found the broken bit of fence that always gave way when she pushed against it. Once you were in, you couldn't get out, because the fence didn't push in the other direction. But Rosie didn't mind that. She knew that Kay would be along to collect her soon enough.

"Hello," she neighed, trotting up to Rosamund. She sniffed the air and whinnied with pleasure at the apple smell. "Is it all right if I . . . ?"

"Help yourself!" Rosamund whinnied back.

Rosie headed for the far corner of the field, where the apple tree was. While Rosie was munching away, Rosamund started trotting across the field towards the gate. Rosie turned to see why.

She stiffened as she saw a familiar horsebox parked outside

the gate. The same man that had taken Rosie was standing there, holding out a carrot to Rosamund.

"No!" Rosie whinnied. "Keep away, Rosamund!"

Just then, the man brought out a loop of rope from behind his back. He threw it over Rosamund's head.

"Rosamund! Don't go with him!" Rosie whinnied. She started to gallop down the field as fast as she could, wishing she hadn't eaten so many apples.

The man flicked a whip and Rosamund leaped out into the lane.

"Help!" Rosamund whickered, sounding frightened.

Rosie tried to gallop faster as

Rosamund was scared into the horsebox by the whip. The man shut the door.

Rosie reached the gate just as the man leaped into the front seat beside his friend. The van screeched away.

"STOP!" Rosie whinnied.

She galloped after the horsebox as it swerved along the lane, gathering speed.

They passed Rosie's field, where Nellie looked up from munching grass and stared in amazement.

"Haven't got time to explain!" Rosie neighed.

They went on towards the school, where everyone was out in the playground for morning break.

"Look, it's Rosie!" someone shouted.

Kay was standing talking to Amy. She looked up to see the horsebox speeding along, followed by Rosie. But the road by the school was narrow and the horsebox was forced to slow down as it passed.

Kay glanced inside the driver's

cab. "It's that man!" she cried. "The one who asked me about Rosie! Quick, let's get the registration number, just in case they're up to something!"

Kay had a good memory for numbers. She repeated the registration number over and over in her head until someone gave her a pen to write it down. Then she went to find Mr Gibb.

As soon as Mr Gibb heard what had happened he said, "Come on. Let's go and fetch Rosie back."

Just then, Amy's mum turned up at the school gates, looking worried. Miss Perkins, the teacher on playground duty, went over to talk to her. Then they both came over to Amy.

"Amy, love, I'm afraid that Rosamund has disappeared from her field," her mum explained.

Kay and Amy looked at each other.

"That horsebox!" Amy gasped. "Do you think . . . ?"

"Come on," said Mr Gibb, grimly. "Let's get Rosie. Then I think we'd better make a trip to the police station."

Miss Perkins nodded her agreement, and Kay and Amy rushed out of the school gates, after Mr Gibb.

Rosie was waiting further along the road.

"Poor Rosie!" Kay said, rushing up to give Rosie a hug. "You look exhausted!"

*

At the police station, Amy went inside with Mr Gibb to give Sergeant Hughes a description of Rosamund. Then she waited outside with Rosie while Kay went in to tell him the registration number of the horsebox that had rushed past. She also described the suspicious man she had seen.

Sergeant Hughes put out a radio call for the horsebox to be stopped. Then he congratulated Kay on her quick thinking in taking down the number.

"It wasn't my quick thinking, it was Rosie's," Kay answered, proudly. "If she hadn't chased the horsebox, it would have driven past the school without us suspecting anything!"

"Do you think you'll catch the thieves?" Mr Gibb asked.

"I should think so," Sergeant Hughes replied. "They can't have got far!"

Kay and Mr Gibb went outside to tell Amy what was happening.

"We'd better take Rosie back to her field now," Kay said.

"Sergeant Hughes said he'd phone the school if there's any news."

They made their way back along the lane leading to Rosie's field. But just as they reached the gate, Sergeant Hughes passed them in his police car. He was smiling.

"I thought I'd come and tell you the good news," he said. "That horsebox has been stopped by our lads in the next village. I'm on my way over there now. And – there's a pony inside who sounds like she's your Rosamund!"

"*YES*!" Kay and Amy both cheered.

Rosie let out a happy snort. "Hurrah!"

"You'd think that pony

understood what we were saying," Sergeant Hughes said, shaking his head.

"Of course she understands!" Kay replied, stroking Rosie's nose.

Sergeant Hughes drove off, and Mr Gibb turned to open the gate.

"Mmm . . ." he said, thoughtfully. "No wonder Rosie's been escaping so much lately. This new catch needs adjusting. I had the same trouble with one of the school gates a while ago."

He looked at Kay. "Tell your dad I'll come and show him how to fix it at the weekend. But in the meantime, you should tie the gate with some rope after you shut it. That'll stop Rosie's tricks – for a while at any rate!" He turned to

Rosie, whose ears had pricked up. "What do you think of that then, Miss?"

Rosie flicked her mane crossly and let out a very rude snort: "Spoilsport!" Then she turned her back on Mr Gibb and swished her tail at him as if he were a fly she wanted to get rid of.

While Kay and Amy were laughing, Nellie came over to see what all the fuss had been about.

Rosie explained proudly how she'd helped save Rosamund.

"Well done!" Nellie neighed. "Though it seems like your travels are over, now," she added, watching Mr Gibb fiddle with the catch on the gate.

But Rosie wasn't listening. She had just spotted a very promising gap in the hedge . . .

Collect all of JENNY DALE'S PONY TALES™!

The prices shown below are correct at the time of going to press. However, Macmillan Publishers reserves the right to show new retail prices on covers which may differ from those previously advertised.

JENNY DALE'S PONY TALES™		
Sam the School Pony	0 330 37468 0	£2.99
Charlie the Champion Pony	0 330 37469 9	£3.99
Lottie the Little Pony	0 330 37472 9	£2.99
Shadow the Secret Pony	0 330 37473 7	£2.99
Rosie the Runaway Pony	0 330 37474 5	£3.50
Willow the Wild Pony	0 330 37475 3	£2.99
